To: _____

From: _____

Nana Says
I Will
Be
Famous
One Day

To my mom, the best Nana ever, and to my aunts,
Margie, Mary, Teresa, Barbara, and Ag

A. S.

For Mum (aka Nana) and for my own nana,
with much love to both

A. J.

Text copyright © 2020 by Ann Stott
Illustrations copyright © 2020 by Andrew Joyner

First edition 2020

Library of Congress Catalog Card Number pending
ISBN 978-0-7636-9560-6

20 21 22 23 24 25 CCP 10 9 8 7 6 5 4 3 2 1

Printed in Shenzhen, Guangdong, China

This book was typeset in Alice.
The illustrations were created digitally.

Candlewick Press
99 Dover Street
Somerville, Massachusetts 02144

visit us at www.candlewick.com

Nana Says I Will Be Famous One Day

Ann Stott

illustrated by Andrew Joyner

CANDLEWICK PRESS

Nana was my very first word.

My whole life, Nana has been my biggest fan.

She comes to all my games and school events.

I can usually find her in the front row.

My mom says I get my athletic ability from my nana. She was a star basketball player and one of the toughest basketball referees around.

She's won the tennis tournament at the senior center three years in a row!

Nana always wants a copy of my swim team schedule as soon as it's out.

She plans her hair appointments around my home meets.

At one swim meet, I had to ask her to move over a little so my team could fit along the side of the pool.

"There's plenty of room for all of us!" she said.

And then she made sure I was first in line.

When I told her I couldn't do the dog paddle, she said,
"Oh YES you can!"

In the fall, she pulled her chair right up to the sideline, as close to the fifty-yard line as possible, so she could give the football coach some tips on how to run the flea-flicker play.

At my spring concert, she danced in the aisle. She said I was so good, I should have had my own solo part.

Every year, Nana buys all my paintings at the school art auction.

She says I will be famous one day.

At my baseball games, Nana has no problem letting the umpire know when he makes a bad call.

"THAT WAS A STRIKE! YOU NEED TO GET YOUR EYES CHECKED!" she yells.

My mom always has to remind her to read the sportsmanship rules that are posted on the backstop.

If my picture is in the local paper, she cleans out the newsstands before lunch.

I'm not sure what she does with all those newspapers.

Last week, she took a tumble at my basketball game trying to get a front-row seat in the school gym. She had to go to the nurse's office. Maybe my mom's right—I do get my speed from her!

The nurse said she needed to rest for a few days.
"NO physical activity!"

My nana was not very happy about that.

"I'm fit as a fiddle," she said.

She was so mad that she had missed my three-point
shot and had to be taken out in a wheelchair.

Every day after school I went to visit my nana. I made her favorite tea, peppermint.

"One lump or two?" I asked her.

When she needed her glasses, I found them for her.

When she wanted to make cookies,

I convinced her to split a chocolate bar instead.

I helped her with chores.

We played crazy eights.

She always has to win.

When I visited her yesterday, she said, "I have a new yoga pose to show you!" Then she slid into the downward dog position.

I reminded her, "NO physical activity!" and helped her to her chair.

"I can't just sit around here all day doing nothing!" she complained.

"Oh yes you can!" I told her.

She has a fan to cheer her on.

Me!